In at the Deep End

T

David Orme

Published in 2002 by:
Nelson Thornes Ltd
Delta Place
27 Bath Road
CHELTENHAM
GL53 7TH
United Kingdom

02 03 04 05 06 / 10 9 8 7 6 5 4 3 2 1

A catalogue record for this book is available from the British Library

ISBN 0-7487-6416-X

Illustrations by Francis Bacon
Cover illustration by Richard Garland (represented by Advocate)
Page make-up by Peter Nickol

Printed and bound in Great Britain by T. J. International

Contents

Chapter 1

Night swim

"Great! It's the right key!"

Toby opened the gate and the three boys went through silently. They all knew that swimming in the school pool at night was against the rules. There would be big trouble if they were caught.

Toby had found the key – the swimming teacher must have dropped it. Toby had dared his best friends Tim and Richard to go with him to the pool that night.

Richard wasn't keen at first. He swam for the city swimming team and didn't want to get into trouble. The other two had talked him into it in the end.

The pool was an outdoor one. There was just enough moonlight for the boys to see. They got changed quickly.

"Don't dive in," whispered Richard. "It'll make a splash."

The three boys slipped quietly into the water and started swimming about. The water seemed warmer than usual – probably because the air was cold at night.

Tim and Toby were happy to muck about. They dived down, then came up again, trying to dunk each other under the water. Richard wished they wouldn't make so much noise.

He thought he might as well put in some practice. He did a couple of warm-up lengths first. Then he switched to backstroke. This was his best stroke.

He set off for the end of the pool, trying to keep his rhythm regular. He knew that this was

sometimes more important than trying to go as fast as possible.

The trouble was, Tim and Toby kept getting in the way. They wanted Richard to stop being so boring and join in the fun.

In the end, Richard decided that he had had enough.

"Come on, you two!" he said. "We've had our swim. Let's get out of here before we get into trouble."

But Tim and Toby didn't want to go.

Chapter 2

Help!

"We've only just got here!" said Toby. "You go if you want!"

Richard really did want to go. He kept thinking about the trouble there would be if they were found out. On the other hand he didn't want to leave his friends. He fooled around with the others for a while, then decided to go.

"I'm off then. You stay if you want."

He got out of the pool, and quickly dried himself on his towel. He was rushing, and wasn't really dry when he got dressed. It was

hard to pull his clothes on over his wet skin.

He walked down to the end of the pool to see Tim. Toby had swum off by himself down to the deep end. Suddenly Toby started to splutter and shout.

"Help! I've got cramp! It's really bad! I can't get to the side!"

Richard knew that cramp could be serious when you were swimming. He always warmed up properly before swimming to make sure it

didn't happen to him.

Tim couldn't help. He was at the wrong end of the pool. In any case, Richard knew what to do. He had been on a life-saving course. This trained people how to save swimmers who were having problems. Lifesavers had to be able to swim even if they were wearing clothes.

Richard ran to the side of the pool and dived in. Toby was splashing about in the middle. Richard reached him and supported him from behind. He towed him to the side, keeping his head above water.

Tim had arrived by now. Between them they got Toby out of the water. Just then Richard saw that they were both laughing. He realised that they had set him up. Toby hadn't been in trouble at all. Now he would have to walk home in soaking wet clothes.

"You stupid idiots!" Richard yelled. But Toby and Tim couldn't stop giggling.

Richard was about to say something even ruder when all three boys froze. A voice boomed at them from the gate.

"And what do you boys think you are doing?"

Chapter 3

A bad day

Richard, Toby and Tim were in a lot of trouble. The booming voice was the head teacher, Mr Parsons. He had been at a late meeting at school, and had heard them as he walked towards the car park.

He took them back to the school and rang their parents. He asked them to come and collect the boys. The boys' parents were not pleased to hear what they had been up to. They did not enjoy getting a lecture from Mr Parsons about being responsible parents. Richard's parents did not shout at him. They just said

17

how disappointed they were. That made it worse.

The next day Richard, Toby and Tim had to see Mr Parsons again. Mrs Constance, their head of year, was with him. Mr Parsons gave them another lecture about being responsible. Richard seemed to get most of the blame, even though it hadn't been his idea.

"You of all people should know the risks of being in the pool without supervision," he said. "I hope you're ashamed of yourself."

He glared at the three boys.

"You are all suspended from school for three days. Luckily for you, Mrs Constance has spoken well of you. Otherwise, I might have removed you from the school altogether."

Richard felt depressed all day. He knew he had been very stupid. It was swimming practice for the city team that evening. He did not really feel like it. He knew he had to try, though.

The practice was at the leisure centre.

Richard got there early and started to get changed. He wanted to warm up thoroughly before the practice.

When he came out of the changing room he met Mike Simmons. Mike was the city team coach. He did not look in a good mood.

"I've just heard about your stupid behaviour last night," he said. " Good swimmers like you need to be specially responsible. A swimming team isn't just about swimming. It's about looking after other people in the team."

Richard knew from Mike's face that something really bad was coming next.

"I'm not interested in having people who behave stupidly in my team. Get dressed and go home."

Chapter 4

Mike strikes a deal

Richard's parents were very upset when he got home. They knew that he didn't usually behave in a stupid way. They thought that Mike Simmons had been very harsh. They knew how important swimming was to Richard. They were worried that this would make him give it up altogether. This would be a great shame, as Richard had a lot of talent.

"Can't you ring him up and talk to him?" said Richard. "I'm sure he'll listen to you."

"You got into this mess, so you must get out of it," said Richard's dad. "I suggest you go up

23

to your room now and write two letters. Write one to Mr Parsons, saying how sorry you are and that you have learnt a lesson. And don't blame anyone else or make excuses. Then write one to Mr Simmons. Tell him that you understand how he feels about what you did. Ask him if there is anything you can do to get back in the team. You never know. He might change his mind."

Richard didn't think it would work. He thought his swimming days were finished. He agreed to write the letters, though. At least it would keep his parents happy. At the moment, he needed as many people on his side as possible.

Two days later Richard got a phone call from Mike Simmons. He asked Richard to meet him at the leisure centre that evening.

"Bring your swimming things," he said.

Richard was puzzled. It was the wrong night for team practice. When he got to the pool he found a lot of young children splashing about.

"I'm glad you wrote me that letter," said Mike. "It's made me think again. You could get back on the team, but you've got to prove that you are responsible."

"How can I do that?" Richard asked eagerly.

"I'm short of a lifesaver for the under-nines swimming club. You're a lifesaver. Help me out here for a few weeks and I'll think again about the team. Is it a deal?"

"It's a deal!"

Chapter 5

A cunning plan

Life-saving for the under nines was very boring. Richard had to sit in a special chair looking down on the pool. He had to watch the children all the time. At first he expected there would be regular action. He imagined himself diving into the pool to rescue someone quite often. He thought about how brave he would look, and how pleased the parents of the rescued child would be. Maybe they would come up with a cash reward!

The weeks went by, and no one needed saving. Mike Simmons had taught them well.

They were all good swimmers. The only good thing was that at the end of the session Richard was able to put in some practice. Mike usually stayed on to give a bit of coaching.

Richard was back at school by now. He was still friends with Toby and Tim. He knew it was no good blaming them for all the trouble. It was his fault just as much as theirs.

"Mike Simmons said I might get back in the team a couple of weeks ago, but since then he hasn't said any more about it. I wish I could do something to show him how responsible I am," Richard said to his friends.

Toby didn't say anything. He felt guilty about what had happened to Richard. He wanted to help.

When Toby got home he had a long talk with his little brother Sam. Sam was in the under-nines' swimming club and was a good swimmer. Like Toby, he was always ready to get involved in things, even if he got into trouble.

"OK," said Sam. "I'll do it. But it's going to cost you!"

Toby sighed. His little brother was too smart sometimes.

Chapter 6

Another rescue

Richard sat in the life-saver's chair for another session. He was beginning to think he would never get back into the team.

Mike Simmons came in and the under nines all jumped into the pool. He allowed them a few minutes to splash around for fun before the serious teaching began.

At last Mike blew his whistle.

"You lot jump into the pool like sacks of spuds!" he said. "Today we're going to teach you to dive!"

Richard watched as the children got out of

the pool. Mike showed them the right position for a simple dive. They all had a go. Some were better than others.

It was Sam's turn. He dived in. When he came to the surface, he was splashing about, and looked like he was in trouble.

Sam sank under the water again. Without hesitating Richard dived in. He reached Sam and pulled him back to the side. Sam stopped struggling straight away. Mike whistled all of the others out of the pool.

Mike helped Sam out of the water. It was just then that Richard realised that something was wrong.

Like his brother, Sam couldn't help giggling! Richard groaned inside. Another trick!

Mike did not look pleased. "Did you set this up, Richard? Is this another one of your stunts? Did you think it would impress me?"

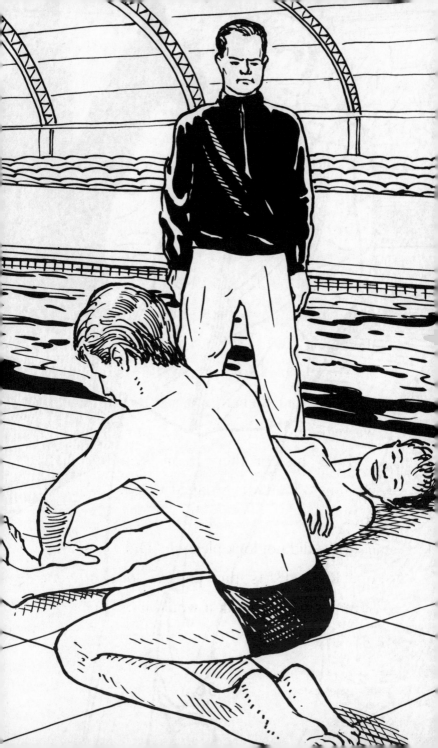

Chapter 7

"You didn't believe me..."

Richard was so angry he could barely speak.

"I didn't know anything about it!" he said at last. But Mike didn't look as if he believed him.

At the end of the session he got changed quickly and set off for home. No one believed anything he said. It just wasn't worth the effort.

At home, he couldn't speak to his parents. He stamped up to his room and shut the door with a bang.

Half an hour later the phone rang.

Richard's mother knocked on his door.

"It's Mr Simmons," she said. "He wants to talk to you."

"I don't want to talk to him. Tell him I've given up swimming for good."

She went downstairs and spoke on the phone. Then Richard's dad came up.

"Richard, don't be so rude. Come and talk to Mr Simmons now," he said angrily.

Unwillingly, Richard went downstairs. He picked up the phone.

"Your mum says you are giving up swimming for good. That right?"

"Yes."

"Well, that's a shame. I was just going to put you back in the team. I had a long talk with Sam after the session. Seems he cooked up the whole scheme with that brother of his."

"You didn't believe me when I said I didn't know," Richard said.

Mike paused.

"That's true. Trouble is, it takes a long time to rebuild trust. I'm sorry I doubted you. Now, it's training tomorrow. Will you be there?"

Richard forgot all his bad feelings. Swimming was all he really wanted to do.

"I'll be there," he said.

Sports ZONE

If you like this book, you may also enjoy others from the same series.

Up For It! (Football)
Trail Bikes (Mountain biking)
Snow Trek (Snowboarding)
Hot Skates (Ice hockey)
Head to Head (Sprint relay)
A Crazy Sport (Triathlon)

Rock Face (Rock climbing)
Speed Bikes (Speedway)
Running into Trouble (Marathon)
Skating to Danger (Outdoor skating)
Hit It! (Water skiing)
Goalie's Nightmare (Football)

Match Ref (Football – coaching, refereeing)
Dive and Survive (Sea diving)
Pit Stop (Formula 1)
Deep Trouble (Potholing)
In at the Deep End (Swimming)
Close to the Wind (Windsurfing)